Tiddlers

Henry's Favourite Friend

by Jane Simmons

W

WALTHAM FOREST LIBRARIES

D0433049

Notes on the series

TIDDLERS are structured to provide support for children who are starting to read on their own. The stories may also be used for sharing with children.

Starting to read alone can be daunting. **TIDDLERS** help by listing the words in the book for a check before reading, and by providing visual support and repeating words and phrases. These books will both develop confidence and encourage reading and rereading for pleasure.

If you are reading this book with a child, here are a few suggestions:

1. Make reading fun! Choose a time to read when you and the child are relaxed and have time to share the story.
2. Talk about the story before you start reading. Look at the cover and the blurb. What might the story be about? Why might the child like it?
3. Look also at the list of words below - can the child tackle most of the words?
4. Encourage the child to retell the story, using the jumbled picture puzzle.
5. Give praise! Remember that small mistakes need not always be corrected.

Here is a list of the words in this story.

Common words:

all	his	to
but	likes	with
her		

Other words:

bark	friends	Sam
best	Henry	sit
breakfast	meow	sleep
dinner	park	
favourite	play	

Henry likes breakfast with Sam.

Henry likes to bark.

Sam likes to meow.

Henry likes to play ...

... with his friends.

Sam likes to sit ...

... with her friends.

Henry likes dinner
with Sam.

But best of all,
Henry likes to sleep ...

... with his favourite
friend, Sam.

Puzzle Time

a

b

Can you find these
pictures in the story?

Which pages are the pictures from?

Turn over for answers

Answers

The pictures come from these pages:

a. pages 10-11

b. pages 6-7

c. pages 12-13

d. pages 18-19

First published in 2012 by
Franklin Watts
338 Euston Road
London
NW1 3BH

Franklin Watts Australia
Level 17/207 Kent Street
Sydney
NSW 2000

Text and illustrations © Jane Simmons 2012

The rights of Jane Simmons as the author
and illustrator of this Work have been
asserted in accordance with the Copyright,
Designs and Patents Act, 1988.

All rights reserved. No part of this
publication may be reproduced, stored
in a retrieval system, or transmitted in
any form or by any means, electronic,
mechanical, photocopy, recording or
otherwise, without the prior written
permission of the copyright owner.

A CIP catalogue record for this book is
available from the British Library.

ISBN 978 1 4451 0683 0 (hbk)
ISBN 978 1 4451 0689 2 (pbk)

Series Editor: Jackie Hamley
Editor: Melanie Palmer
Series Advisor: Catherine Glavina
Series Designer: Peter Scoulding

Printed in China

Franklin Watts is a division of Hachette Children's Books,
an Hachette UK company. www.hachette.co.uk